ZUGGY
🐾 SPOOKY OOKY STORIES 🐾

RESCUE PUG

JEAN MARIE ALFIERI

Zuggy the Pug – Spooky Ooky Stories
Written by Jean Marie Alfieri
Illustrations by Alexandra Ruiz
Graphic Design and Layout by Christine Sterling-Bortner

Copyright 2021 All rights reserved.

No part of this story or book may be reproduced, stored in a retrieval system, or transmitted in any form or by any means, electronic, mechanical, copying, recording, or otherwise, without the written permission of the author.
Printed in the U.S.A.

All Rights Reserved   First Edition

Dedication

To those of us who enjoy the thrill of being scared
– and a great dog hero – any time of year!
~ JMA

To my mom, Nerissa, my brother Nikolai, my sister, Natasha, and my friends for all their love and support.
~ AR

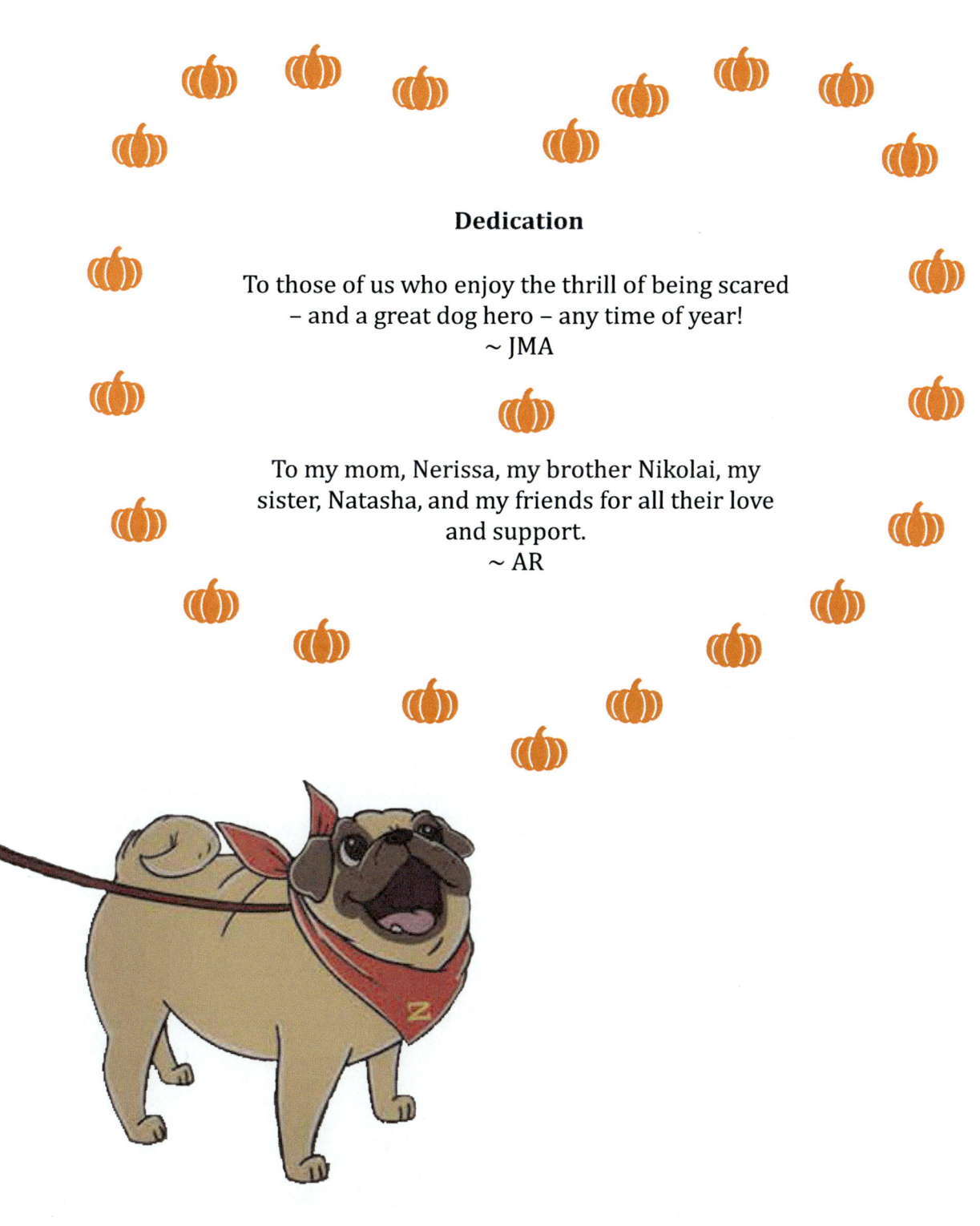

LIST OF STORIES

The Whispering Ghost

Secrets of the Haunted Barn

Fright Night

The Whispering Ghost

There was talk around town
About the red barn.
Kids whispered of hauntings
Out at the old farm.

Its color had faded.
Its boards had come loose.
The ceiling had fallen
Where hens used to roost.

Odd shadows and figures.
Mysterious sounds.
Trash cans toppled over
And strewn all around.

Zuggy trotted back home
That crisp Autumn day.
He cut through the farm as
The sun slipped away.

Then came a cold drizzle.
White clouds turned to grey.
He was passing the barn
And thought, "Should I stay?"

The rickety barn door
Swung loose from its hinge.
The whole front was leaning.
It made Zuggy cringe.

He snuck in on tiptoe.
Thick dust made him cough.
He thought he heard scratching
Up in the dark loft.

A crow in the rafters
Looked down from her nest.
The bird glared at Zuggy
Like he was a pest.

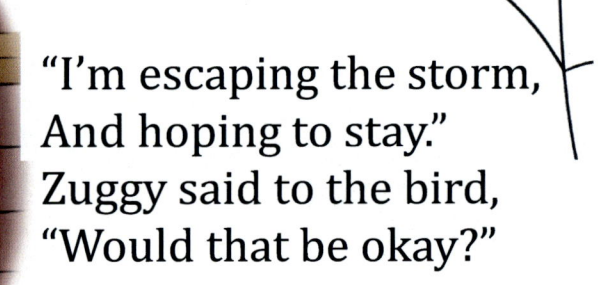

"I'm escaping the storm,
And hoping to stay."
Zuggy said to the bird,
"Would that be okay?"

"It is far from okay,"
The crow squawked at him.
She ruffled her feathers,
All angry and grim.

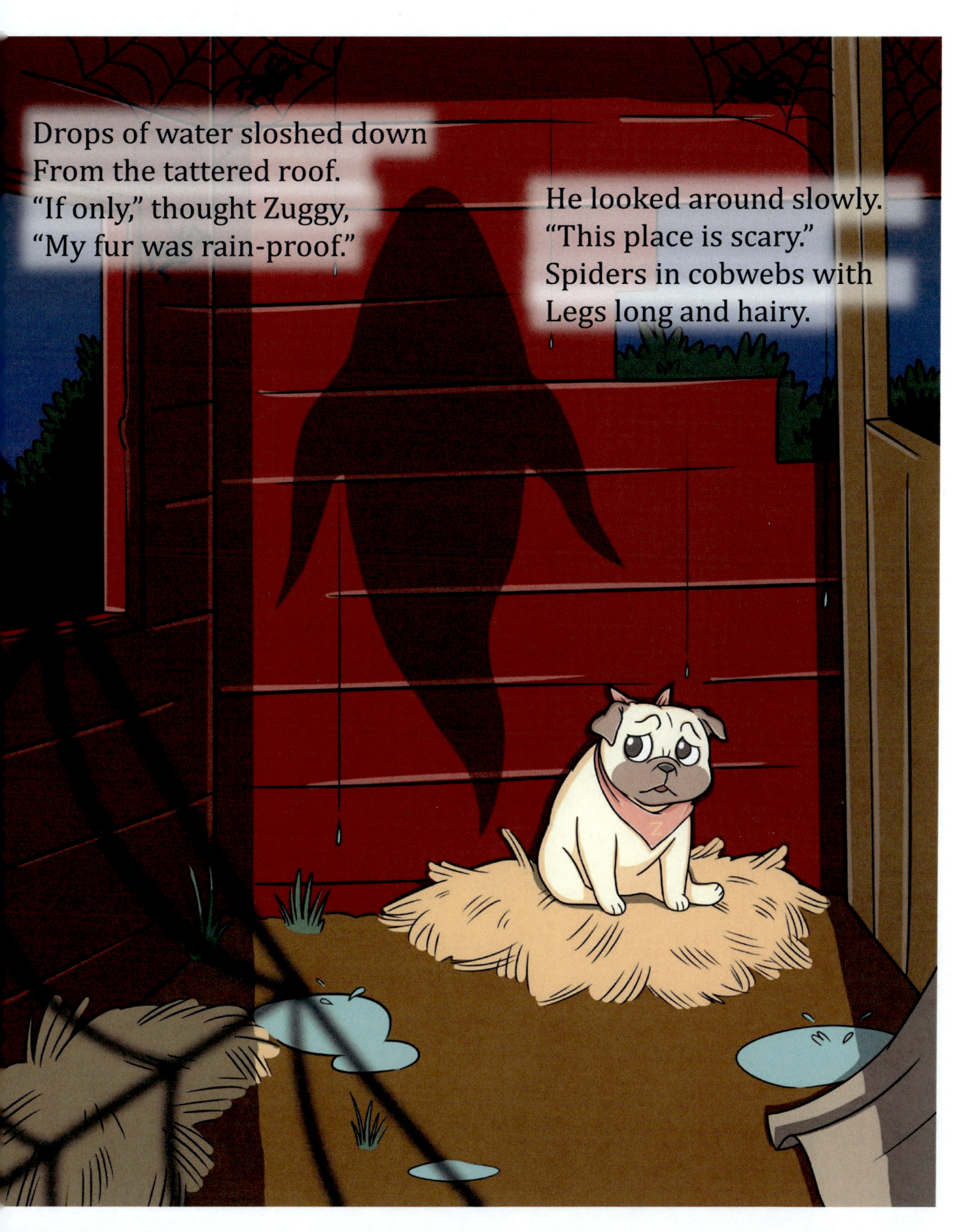

A white ghostly figure,
Its movement a blur,
Swooped down from the rafters
And wisped through his fur.

It swirled 'round the barn.
It called him by name.
Was this a weird trick?
Or some twisted game?

Secrets of the Haunted Barn

Zuggy woke the next day.
His fur finally dry.
He'd escaped from the barn.
He held his head high.

The sun bright and warm.
The clouds far away.
The kids had a new kite.
He watched as they played.

It soared ever higher.
They held the string tight.
Then a swift gust of wind
Snapped up the kids' kite!

Zuggy barked to the kids,
"I'll track down that kite."
It dipped a bit lower.
But still was in flight.

Dodging cornstalks and weeds
To chug after that kite,
Zuggy had to run fast
To keep it in sight.

He skidded to a stop
And barked with alarm.
The kite had crash landed
Back at the old farm!

Flapping and fluttering,
He saw the kite tail.
The fabric was snagged
On a sharp rusty nail.

In the cracked window was
A strange ghostly blur.
Zuggy suddenly felt
A chill down his fur.

The barn door creaked open.
Beyond it was dark.
He took a deep breath and
Marched in with a "Bark!"

He climbed up the worn stairs
And almost slipped off
When somewhere behind him
He heard a loud cough!

Zuggy backed down the steps.
He eased toward the door,
Stopped near a horse stall
And sniffed the dirt floor.

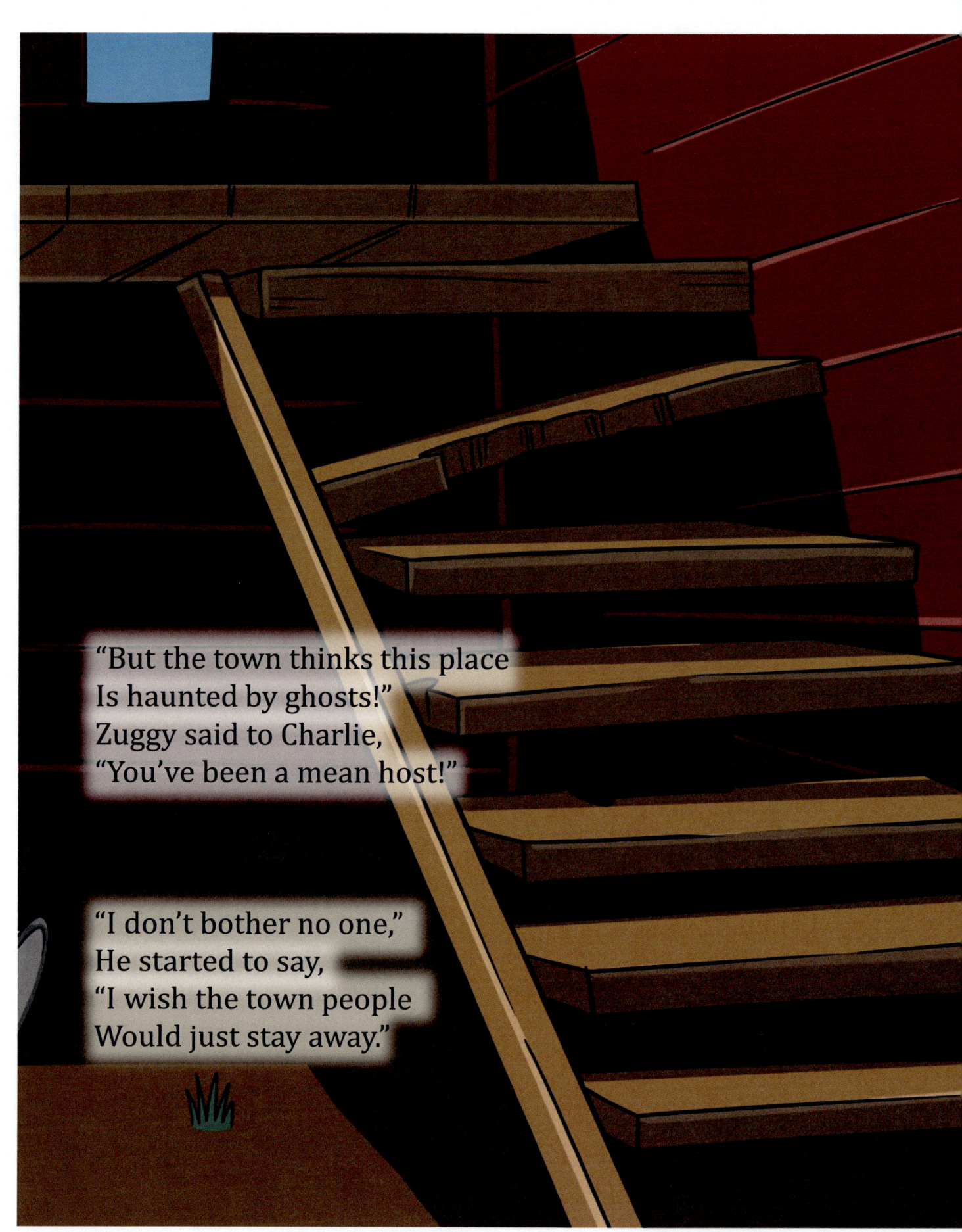

Zuggy didn't reply,
Lost in his own thought.
He stared at the window.
The kite was still caught.

"We'll get that," said Charlie,
Following his gaze.
"Watch your step and stay close.
This place is a maze."

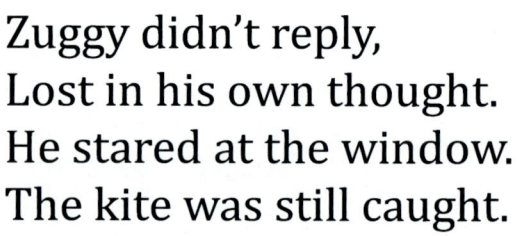

"Be careful over there."
Some broken glass gleamed.
They climbed up wobbly stairs,
Then over a beam.

They pulled in the kite and
Went out the same way.
Charlie shook Zuggy's paw
And asked him to stay.

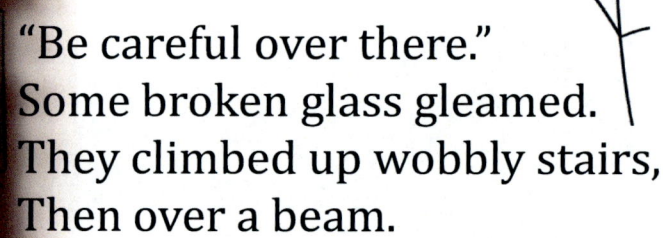

They looked at each other.
"Charlie, what was that?"
"Don't know," Charlie sputtered,
"Could it be a bat?"

Their eyes glued to the door,
They both backed away.
"Let's solve this," said Zuggy,
"Let's do it today!"

"When I count to three,
Let's bust through the door,"
"And then," whispered Zuggy,
"Let's shout a big 'Roar'!"

ROOOAAAARRR!!!

"Who are you?" asked Zuggy.
"The cat in the barn.
I keep people away
By haunting the farm!"

"Don't forget about us!"
They all turned to see,
Two rats dusting off in
The shade of a tree.

"And who might you be?"
Zuggy had to ask.
"Professional Haunters.
It's no easy task!"

"Oh please, give me a break!"
The cat rolled her eyes.
"I could haunt this whole place
Without you two guys!"

Before they could argue,
Zuggy waved good-bye.
"Guess I won't be alone,"
Charlie said with a sigh.

Zuggy was happy
Their secret was out.
They'd all soon be friends.
He hadn't a doubt!

The dare started at school.
The kids thought it funny.
To prove they were brave.
Not a wager of money.

Roy and Pearl agreed,
And they wouldn't back down.
They just wished it wasn't
The spookiest place in town.

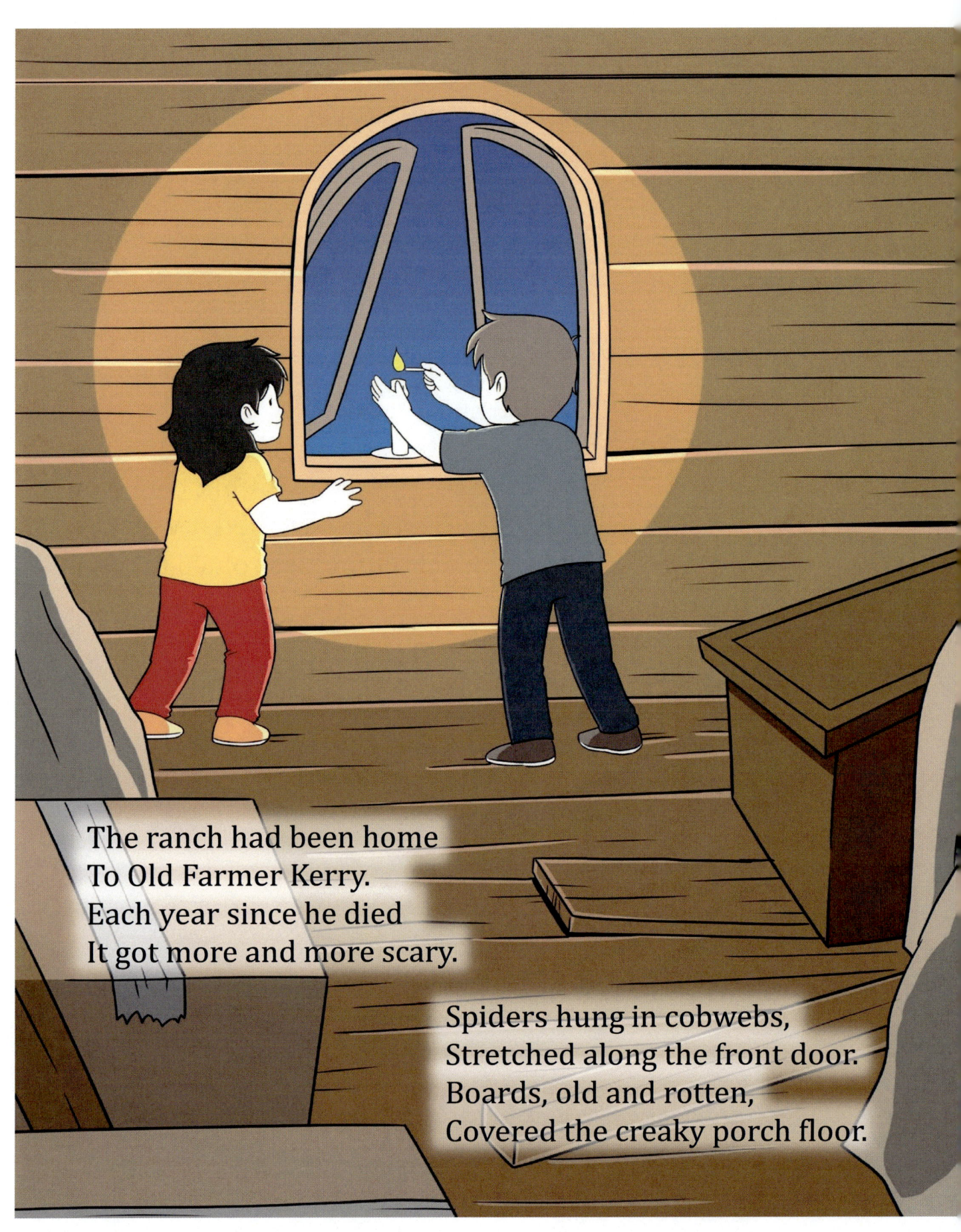

The ranch had been home
To Old Farmer Kerry.
Each year since he died
It got more and more scary.

Spiders hung in cobwebs,
Stretched along the front door.
Boards, old and rotten,
Covered the creaky porch floor.

Windows panes were shattered.
Torn drapes blew in the air.
Going after dark?
It was the ultimate dare.

Once inside the sad house
The kids would have to creep.
Up the old staircase
Without uttering a peep.

Once they reached the attic
They would almost be through.
Lighting a candle,
Would be the last thing to do.

It was chilly that evening.
Stormy clouds filled the sky.
The kids left the house
Without saying "Good-bye."

Zuggy followed behind.
The kids didn't see him.
Their flashlight flickered,
Then its hazy light went dim.

A tremble filled Pearl's voice.
"Can you make out the way?"
Roy peered up ahead,
"I'm trying but can't quite say."

A crow cried behind them.
Rustling leaves on the branch.
They panicked and ran
Down the dark path to the ranch.

The kids slid to a stop
By the cobwebby door.
Their eyes wide with fright.
They were frozen in horror.

The shutters were loose and
Banged around in the breeze.
Pearl's voice was shaky,
"Can we get out of here, please?"

"I've heard there are spiders
With big eyes glowing red.
And their bite," said Roy,
"Could kill an elephant dead!"

Zuggy pranced through a field
Of plump pumpkins and gourds.
Behind the old house
He wiggled through some loose boards.

Calling out to Charlie
Zuggy ran up the stairs.
He had to tell him
About the kids and their dare.

Charlie had been napping
On the living room rug.
He woke up to find
His favorite fun-loving pug!

Not quite a full army,
But Charlie's friend, Moe,
Was helping them build
A live totem-pole!

The barn cat named Alley,
Brought over a candle.
She lit it and then,
Slowly passed off the handle.

Their mission accomplished.
The window filled with light.
While the kids outside
Were shivering with fright.

A big spider dangled.
Pearl couldn't help but stare.
"Roy, can we go home?
I don't care about the dare."

Roy hated to admit
That he felt the same way.
He answered sullenly,
"Sure, sis. Whatever you say."

They turned to walk away,
But then spun back around,
Snuck up to the door
And whispered, "What is that sound?!"

Zuggy's friends ran downstairs,
With a thunderous roar,
Slid on the carpet
Just as Roy opened the door.

In a flurrious blur,
Off the porch they all flew,
Tumbled on the grass,
Through icy patches of dew.

Pearl picked up Zuggy and
Toward the window they turned.
She gasped when she saw
Where the bright candle burned.

Roy stood right beside her,
Not believing his eyes.
The candle was lit.
Such a fabulous surprise!

The kids told the story,
But not one friend at school
Believed that a pug
Could pull off something that cool!

The End

ABOUT THE POET AND HER PUG

Author, Speaker, and Dog Fan, Jean is originally from the Chicagoland area. She currently lives with her husband and their fur-family, which includes a well-pampered adopted senior pug, in Colorado Springs. She enjoys visiting local schools and offering virtual author visits to connect with kids and share her love for dogs and storytelling.

Check out the great photo gallery at: www.ZuggythePug.com and sign up for Zuggy's monthly newsletter to keep up on all their pugnacious adventures.

Jean and her pug LOVE virtual author visits with 1st and 2nd grade classes. Connect with her at: www.JeanAlfieri.com – where pugs and poetry collide!

Want more Zuggy?
Scan the codes!

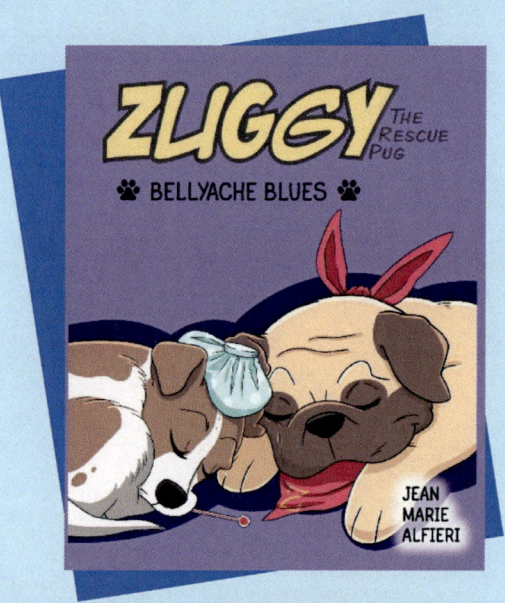

Zuggy the Pug – Bellyache Blues

Check out these Mom's Choice award-winning books. Get your copy (Paperback or Kindle) on Amazon today!

Zuggy the Pug – Adoption Day

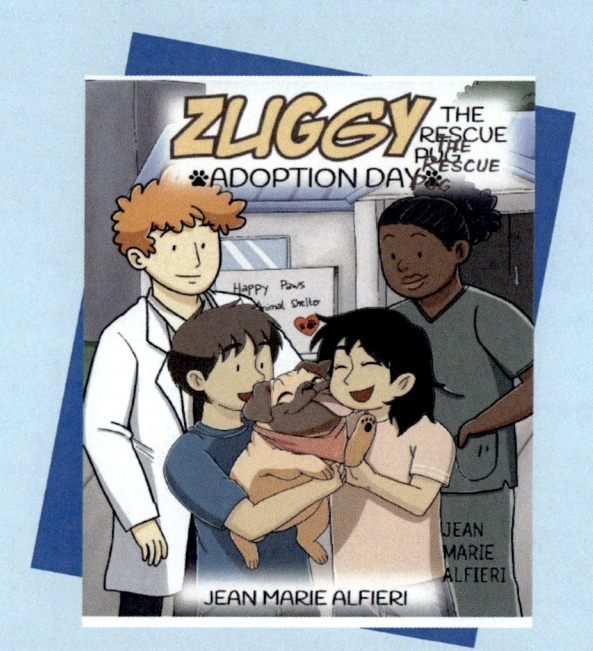

Remember to visit us at ZuggyThePug.com!

Made in the USA
Middletown, DE
08 March 2023